W9-DFD-909

Date: 01/23/12

E NORAC
Norac, Carl.
Monster, don't eat me! /

PALM BEACH COUNTY
LIBRARY SYSTEM
3650 Summit Boulevard
West Palm Beach, FL 33406-4198

Original title: *O monster, eet me niet op!*
Copyright © 2006 by Uitgeverij De Eenhoorn,
Vlasstraat 17, B-8710 Wielsbeke (Belgium)
English translation copyright © 2006 by Elisa Amado
First English edition published in Canada and the USA
by Groundwood Books in 2006.

All rights reserved. No part of this publication may be reprodu-
ced, stored in a retrieval system or transmitted, in any form or
by any means, without the prior written consent of the publisher
or a license from The Canadian Copyright Licensing Agency
(Access Copyright). For an Access Copyright license, visit
www.accesscopyright.ca or call toll free to 1-800-893-5777.

Groundwood Books / House of Anansi Press
110 Spadina Avenue, Suite 801, Toronto, Ontario M5V 2K4
Distributed in the USA by Publishers Group West
1700 Fourth Street, Berkeley, CA 94710

Library and Archives Canada Cataloging in Publication
Norac, Carl
Monster, don't eat me!
by Carl Norac; pictures by Carll Cneut
Translation of: O monster eet me niet op!
ISBN-13: 978-0-88899-800-2
ISBN-10: 0-88899-800-7
I.Cneut, Carll II. Title
PZ7.N76M67 2007   j839.31'364   C2006-903285-8

Printed and bound in Belgium

Monster, Don't Eat Me!

Carl Norac

Pictures by

Carll Cneut

Groundwood Books   House of Anansi Press   Toronto   Berkeley

Alex was a greedy little pig. He loved to eat.

One morning he got up early and snuck out into
the garden. He found some new potatoes. Before
long at least ten had disappeared.

That was when his mother found him.

"There you are," Alex's mother scolded. "Look at
you. Always eating between meals! And you are so
dirty. Go wash up and don't do it again!"

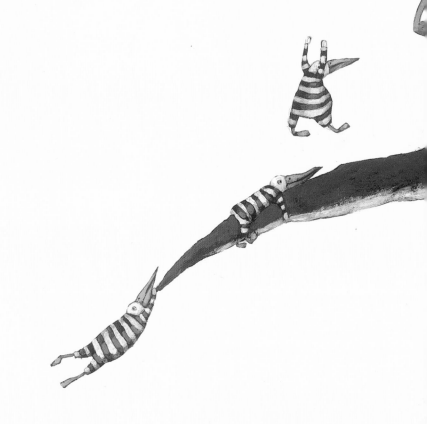

Alex went off to take a bath in the river. His mother was so mean. What are new potatoes for anyway? he thought to himself. I just wanted a little snack.

Along the path he saw an apple tree. It was heavy with shiny, golden apples. But they were hanging out of reach.

Oh well, he thought. I'm not supposed to eat snacks between meals anyway.

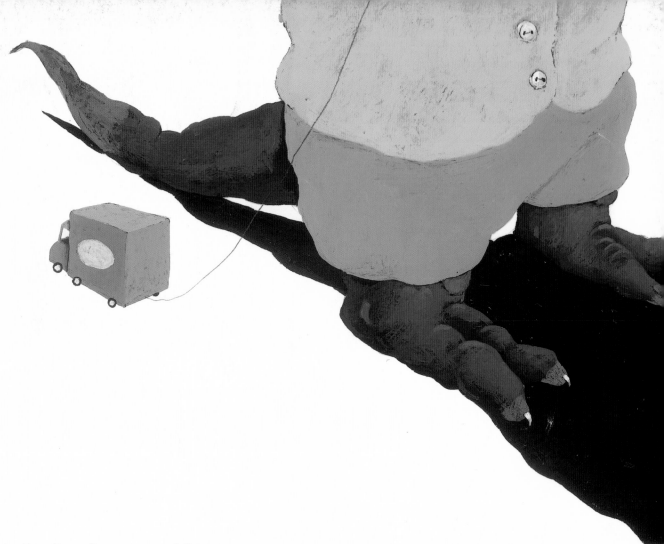

Then a little further on Alex saw an even more enticing sight. The plumpest, shiniest, red raspberries were hanging on a bush at exactly the right height for picking.

Who can resist a raspberry? he asked himself. Not me, that's for sure.

Suddenly, a huge dark shadow loomed over him.

An enormous monster scooped him up and was about to pop poor Alex into his mouth.

"Monster, don't eat me!" cried Alex.

The monster paid no attention. He had spotted the glorious berries.

"Raspberries," he gloated. "The perfect snack. You'll have to wait," he said to Alex. "I'll eat you later."

The monster tucked the little pig into his pocket. Alex fell right to the disgusting, fuzzy bottom. It was dark. He could smell an old wad of bubble gum. He found used candy wrappers, a chewed-up pencil stub and a loose button.

Suddenly, he heard strange rumbling sounds. That's the monster's belly growling, he thought to himself. I'd better get out of here!

But it was too late. Huge fingers were fumbling around in the pocket. They curled around him and he felt himself being plucked up.

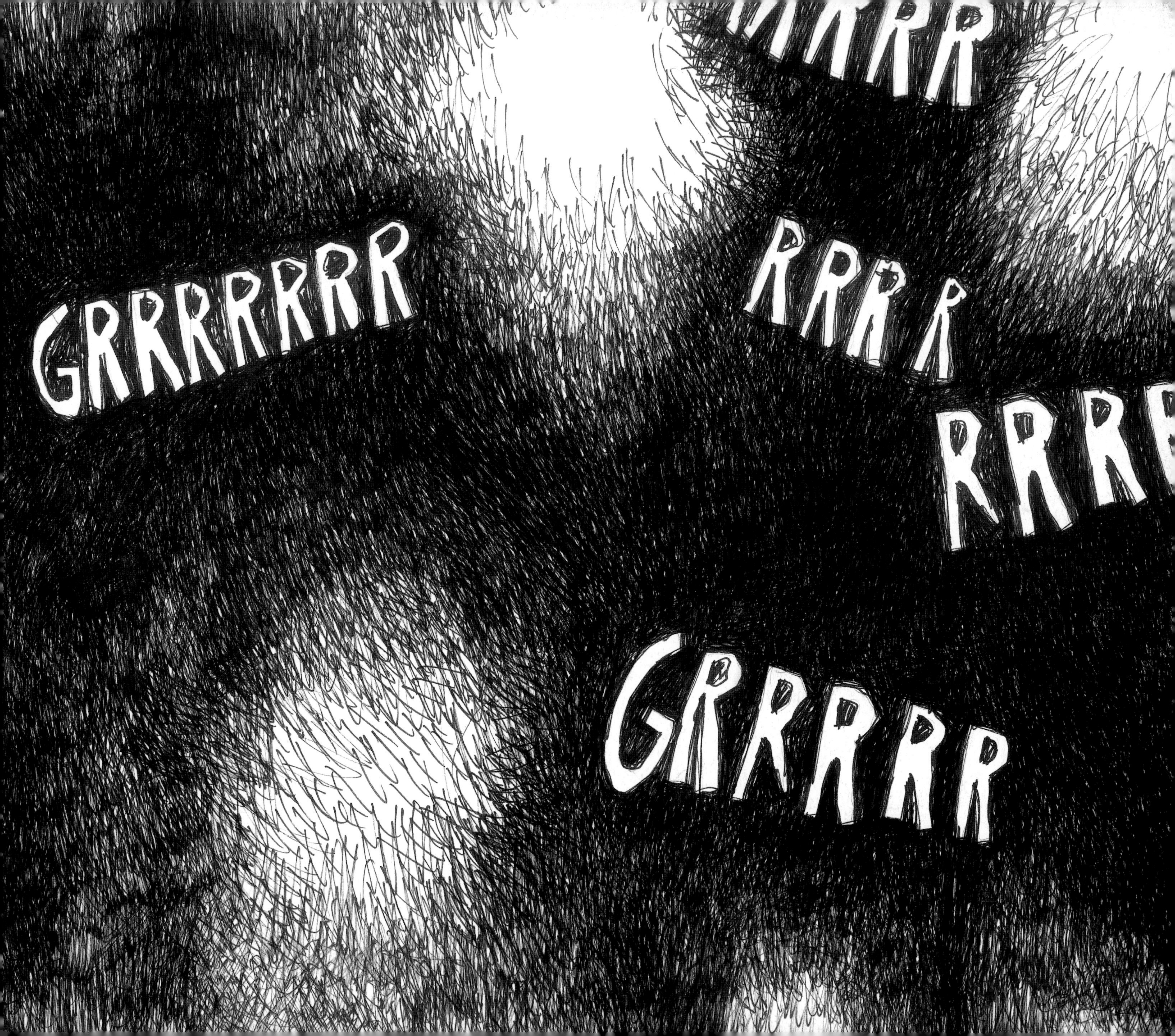
GRRRRRRR
RRRR
GRRRRR

"Monster, don't eat me!" cried Alex.

"Why not?" said the monster laughing.

"Because right near here I saw a baby elephant. He looked really delicious. He's lots fatter than me."

"Yum," slurped the monster.

He tucked Alex under his arm and rushed off through the forest in search of the baby elephant. Alex was shaken up. He had escaped being eaten. But for how long? He'd made up the elephant.

After a while the monster stopped
running. He was out of breath.
"I don't see any fat baby elephant,
little pig. It's your turn now."
"Monster, don't eat me!"
cried Alex. "Can't you see that
cloud?"
"Yes, and so what?" growled the
monster impatiently.
"Well, everyone knows that the Dodu–Dodu lives
on that cloud. He's the most delicious bird in the
world. You'd better hurry or he'll get away."
The monster stuffed Alex back into his pocket
and climbed up a low hill. The cloud was drifting
right overhead. When he jumped for it, he missed
and rolled over in the dust.

"I couldn't catch that Dodu-Dodu," said the monster, brushing himself off. "But at least I've got this little piglet."

"Monster, don't eat me!" cried Alex. "I've got a secret for you."

"What secret is that? Get on with it," growled the monster impatiently.

"Well, under your feet, buried in the ground, there is a secret city. There are lots of tunnels and warrens and at least a thousand rabbits live there."

"You'd better watch out if you're telling me a story. I want a snack now!" grumbled the monster as he shoved Alex back into his pocket.

The monster began to dig a huge hole with his big fingers. But dig and dig as he might, he found nothing more than a few earthworms.

He grabbed Alex angrily and opened his mouth wide.

"Monster, don't eat me!" cried Alex. The monster didn't answer. He opened his mouth even wider.

Suddenly, a really truly huge shadow loomed over them both.

"There you are," the monster's mother scolded. "Look at you. Always eating between meals! And you are so dirty. Go wash up and don't do it again!"

The monster dropped Alex immediately and walked dejectedly over to the river to take a bath. Alex ran off as fast as his shaky legs could carry him.

When he reached his house he saw that everyone was eating breakfast. Alex jumped into his mother's arms and hugged her tight. There would be lots of time later to tell her about what had happened just because she made him take a bath.

Carl Norac

was born in Mons, Belgium. His books have had huge worldwide appeal and have been translated into eighteen languages. He has collaborated with Carll Cneut on several picture books.

Carll Cneut

was born in a small village on the Belgian-French border and has illustrated more than twenty books, many of which have been translated into fifteen languages. He has won numerous awards for his work and has exhibited his art all over the world. He thinks an illustrator is a story-teller. It is his ambition to tell never-ending stories.